Waddle with Scuttle
or
Swim with Kim
In the End the Good Guys Always Win

by Ashley Pickens

Outskirts Press, Inc.
http://www.outskirtspress.com

ISBN: 978-1-4787-5084-0

Outskirts Press and the "OP" logo are trademarks belonging to Outskirts Press, Inc.

PRINTED IN THE UNITED STATES OF AMERICA

This Book Belongs to:

_____

He was trying to find food to eat,
But then he looked down by his feet.

Instead of saying **YUMMY**,
The last place he wanted to put
her was in his tummy.

He said,
"My name is Scuttle and
I love to play, would you like to
be my friend today?"

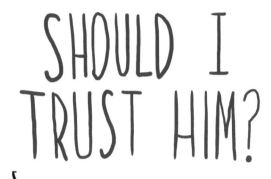

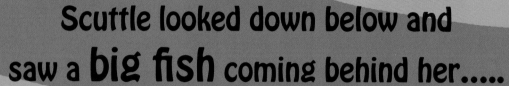

Scuttle looked down below and
saw a **big fish** coming behind her.....

that looked very **mean**.

After this Scuttle knew he had feelings for Kim.
She felt the same when she looked at him.

Scuttle thought his friends would think
she was great,
but to them she was just bait.

When Kim left to go home that night,
Scuttle and his friends **got into a fight.**

They said,
"How could you love a fish
when a fish is our main dish?"

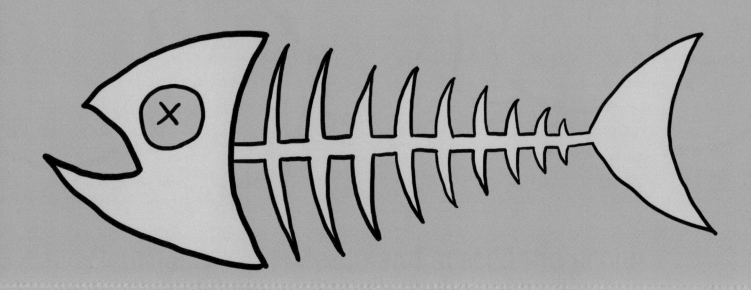

Scuttle waddled off to bed
with thoughts of Kim in his head.

That morning Kim and Scuttle met to play hoping it would be a **good day**.

When all of a sudden six penguins
gathered around,
one grabbed Kim and another pushed
Scuttle to the ground.

Scuttles friends came and scared the group away. The pack left Kim but said, **"We will be back another day."**

Scuttle said,
"Kim I really think we are meant to be, but it's
too dangerous for you to be with me."

While Scuttle tried losing Kim's track,
surely the **bad penguins** did come back.

They came and **took Kim by surprise.**
Eating her was the only thing they needed for a prize.

Scuttle puffed up his chest until he thought it would **POP.**

He spread out his wings and **SPUN** like a top.

What they thought would end in a disaster,
will now be filled with fun and laughter.
They will live happily ever after.

The End.